Nestled on the edge of town
sat a little gift shop.

The Gift Shop Bear

Written and Illustrated
by Phyllis Harris

WORTHY
kids™

Inside the shop, in a dusty attic,
in a cozy box . . .

a little bear listened
to the frosty wind
whistling outside the window.

Each year, Bear watched patiently as the tree outside his window changed with the seasons.

When the last leaf fell, Bear knew Christmas was near. He could feel the cold deep in his stuffing. It was almost time.

One day, the attic floor creaked. Bear's heart raced.

Could it be?

Whoosh!

Bear squinted. Through the dim light, he saw two brown eyes shining like copper pennies.

Annie!

Annie gently lifted Bear from his box and held him close. "I've missed you, Bear," she whispered into his furry ear.

BEAR

Annie carried Bear down the steps to Nana's shop. The scent of fresh-baked gingerbread and pine tickled his nose.

Lights twinkled,
and cheerful ornaments
glimmered in the window.
Bear recognized the soft
sound of his favorite carol.
His heart thumped happily.

Annie tucked Bear in his usual spot beneath the shop's tree. "I'll see you tomorrow, Bear."

Over the next few weeks, Bear and Annie filled the shop with laughter and shared secrets.

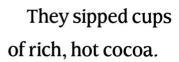

They cut out snowflakes and made paper chains to hang on the tree.

They sipped cups of rich, hot cocoa.

They watched as soft snowflakes floated through the sky,
landing on the carolers who sang outside the shop door.

Bear heard children *ooh* and *aah* when they discovered treasures to add to their wish lists. Many children wanted Bear, but Annie was always quick to say, "Bear is not for sale."

Each night, Annie placed Bear in his
special spot under the tree. The fading light
soothed him to sleep.

"Wake up, Bear! It's Christmas Eve!"
Annie sang out one morning.

Bear and Annie watched as more and
more shoppers arrived.

"I'm going to miss this lovely, old shop,"
Bear heard a customer say to Nana. "I've
been coming here since I was a little girl."

Bear couldn't believe it.
*Could Nana really be
closing the shop?*

The shelves were empty.
The winter sun sat low in the
sky, and Bear shivered as the
door closed behind the last
shopper.

Nana gently lowered Bear
into a box. He wondered if he
would ever see Annie again.

Sitting in the dark box,
Bear squeezed his eyes shut
and thought of his time with
Annie in the cozy little shop.

Bear heard a roar and
a rumble. He tossed and
tumbled.

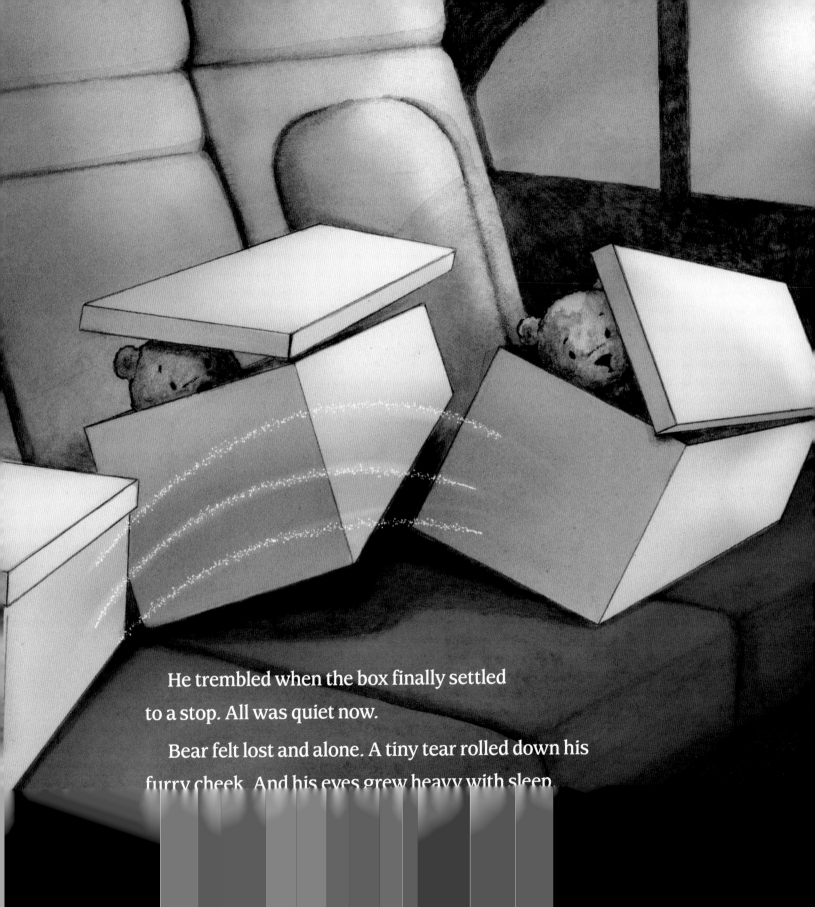

He trembled when the box finally settled
to a stop. All was quiet now.

Bear felt lost and alone. A tiny tear rolled down his
furry cheek. And his eyes grew heavy with sleep.

Bear woke to the sound of
familiar voices. His nose twitched
with the scent of fresh-baked
gingerbread. His ears tingled
as he heard the soft sound of
his favorite Christmas song.

Was that pine he smelled in the air?

Could it be?

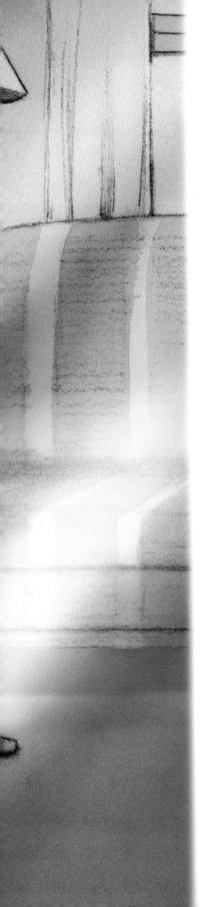

Whoosh!

Bear squinted. He saw two brown eyes shining like copper pennies.

Annie!

"Bear!" shouted Annie. She wrapped him in a warm hug. "I thought I'd lost you."

Nana smiled and said, "Bear is yours now, Annie."

Christmas day came and
went, and Nana put away the
decorations. But this time,
Bear didn't go back to
his box in the attic.

STOCKINGS

WREATHS

Christmas was still
Bear's favorite time of year.

But now he had a place
where he belonged . . .

in every season.